A HOUSE FOR EVERYONE

of related interest

WHO ARE YOU?
The Kid's Guide to Gender Identity
Brook Pessin-Whedbee
Illustrated by Naomi Bardoff
ISBN 978 1 78592 728 7
eISBN 978 1 78450 580 6

VINCENT THE VIXEN
A Story to Help Children Learn about Gender Identity
Alice Reeves
Illustrated by Phoebe Kirk
ISBN 978 1 78592 450 7
eISBN 978 1 78450 826 5
Part of the *Truth & Tails Children's Books* series

ARE YOU A BOY OR ARE YOU A GIRL?
Sarah Savage and Fox Fisher
Illustrated by Fox Fisher
ISBN 978 1 78592 267 1
eISBN 978 1 78450 556 1

THE PRINCE AND THE FROG
A Story to Help Children Learn about Same-Sex Relationships
Olly Pike
ISBN 978 1 78592 382 1
eISBN 978 1 78450 731 2

CAN I TELL YOU ABOUT GENDER DIVERSITY?
A guide for friends, family and professionals
CJ Atkinson
Illustrated by Olly Pike
ISBN 978 1 78592 105 6
eISBN 978 1 78450 367 3
Part of the *Can I tell you about...?* series

MINNIE AND MAX ARE OK!
A Story to Help Children Develop a Positive Body Image
Chris Calland and Nicky Hutchinson
Illustrated by Emmi Smid
ISBN 978 1 78592 233 6
eISBN 978 1 78450 514 1

A HOUSE FOR EVERYONE

A Story to Help Children Learn about
Gender Identity and Gender Expression

JO HiRST

ILLUSTRATED BY NAOMi BARDOFF

Jessica Kingsley Publishers
London and Philadelphia

First published in 2018
by Jessica Kingsley Publishers
73 Collier Street
London N1 9BE, UK
and
400 Market Street, Suite 400
Philadelphia, PA 19106, USA

www.jkp.com

Library of Congress Cataloging in Publication Data
A CIP catalog record for this book is available from the Library of Congress

British Library Cataloguing in Publication Data
A CIP catalogue record for this book is available from the British Library

ISBN 978 1 78592 448 4
eISBN 978 1 78450 823 4

Printed and bound in China

Lunchtime is our favourite part of the day.

"I'll get all the sticks we need," says Ivy. "It won't take long."

She is the fastest runner in our group. She gathers large sticks from all over the playground.

Ivy is a girl. She likes to have her hair cut really short.

Her favourite clothes are shorts and a T-shirt, and she never, ever chooses to wear a dress.

"I'll build the house," says Alex. "I'll make sure it holds together and does not fall down."

Alex loves to build. They have the biggest LEGO® collection of all of our friends.

They take the sticks that Ivy has collected and carefully balance them up against the fence.

"I'll decorate the house," says Sam.
"When I have finished it will look amazing!"

Sam is very artistic and loves putting
different colours together.

He collects flowers and leaves from all the
different plants and trees in the playground.

He drapes them carefully on the house. When
he is finished it looks beautiful.

Sam is a boy. He loves to wear his hair long. His favourite sport is basketball.

Sometimes, when he plays basketball, he wears his hair in a ponytail.

"We will need something to sit on," says Jackson. "I'll take care of that."

Jackson is very, very strong.

He carries the biggest, heaviest rocks from the playground into our house.

The big flat rocks make comfortable seats for everyone.

Jackson is a boy. He loves to wear dresses.
At home he has a huge collection of sparkly shoes.

Dresses are not just for girls. Clothes are for everyone.
We can all wear the clothes that we like.

"What about a sign for visitors?" asks Tom. "I'll make that!"

Tom loves spelling.

He uses small rocks to spell the word "Welcome" at the entrance of our house.

Tom is a boy.

When he was born everyone thought he was a girl. They gave him a girl's name. This made Tom sad.

When he grew up he told everyone he was a boy. Now everyone calls him "he" and "Tom." This makes Tom really happy.

With all of us working together the house is soon ready.

Ivy brings her dinosaur collection into the house. We make a rock mountain for the dinosaurs.

Jackson brings his tiny teddies into the house. We each get to hold one.

Alex brings their LEGO® into the house.
We build a LEGO playhouse for the teddies.

Tom brings his favourite joke book
to the house and tells us some
funny jokes.

Sam brings his basketball to
the house. We go outside and
play basketball for a while.

The house starts to get really crowded but it's lots of fun!

Ivy yells, "To the monkey bars everyone!"

We all love the monkey bars!

Even though we are all a little bit different,
we are still the same and we are all friends.

NOTES FOR GROWN-UPS

A House for Everyone shows children that, while we are all special and unique, we are all the same at heart and can all be friends. It provides an easy way to show children the difference between gender identity and gender expression.

This simple story is a useful tool for helping to break down some of the gender stereotypes that are prevalent in our society and lets all children know it's OK to be themselves.

Life would be pretty boring if we were all the same. Gender diversity is something we can embrace and celebrate.

SUPPORTING CHILDREN

Some children might have a gender expression that doesn't match some of our current gender norms. That might have nothing to do with their gender identity.

Some children might need time to explore their gender identity to work it out.

It's important that all children are free to be themselves. Children need to feel safe and comfortable to thrive, and have the very best mental health and academic outcomes that we can give them.

Gender identity   How you feel *inside* about whether you are a boy or a girl or something else.

Gender expression   How you express yourself on the *outside* through things like clothing, mannerisms and hairstyle.

Transgender   Someone who does not identify with the gender they were assigned at birth Transgender children are insistent, consistent and persistent that their gender identity does not match the gender they were assigned at birth. The character Tom, in the book, is transgender.

Non binary   Someone who does not identify exclusively as male or female. Some transgender children identify as non binary. The character Alex, in the book, is non binary.

Cisgender   Someone who identifies as the gender they were assigned at birth. The characters Ivy, Sam and Jackson, in the book, are cisgender.

TOPICS FOR DISCUSSION

Toys and Games

- Ask the children what games they like to play?

- Can anyone play these games?

- You may like to point out to the children that toys are there for all children to play with. There are no toys that "belong" to girls or boys.

Hair

- Ask the children how they like to wear their hair.

- Can anyone wear their hair like that?

- You may like to point out sports stars/well-known people/adults who have hairstyles that break gender stereotypes.

Clothes

- Ask the children what they like to wear and why. You may like to point out that clothes are for everyone and the important thing is to feel comfortable in them.

LESSON PLAN

Lead a discussion with the children about who they like to play with during their playtime.

- Ask them why they like their friends. What are some of the things their friends are good at? What are the children good at? Are they good at the same things?

- What are some of the things about the children and their friends that are the same? What are some of the things about the children and their friends that are different?

- What are some of the things the children like most about their friends that are different to them?

Using different craft materials, ask the children to make a picture of themselves and a friend playing at playtime. Ask the children to include some of the things they like about their friends that are the same as them and also some of the things they like about their friend that are different to them.

Use these pictures to make a class mural with the heading "We are all the same. We are all different. We are all friends."

FURTHER READING

Gender Born, Gender Made – Dr Diane Ehrensaft

The Gender Creative Child – Dr Diane Ehrensaft

The Transgender Child – Rachel Pepper, Stephanie Brill

Who Are You? The Kid's Guide to Gender Identity – Brook Pessin-Whedbee, Naomi Bardoff

The Gender Fairy – Jo Hirst

The Boy and the Bindi – Vivek Shraya

Are You a Boy or Are You a Girl? – Sarah Savage, Fox Fisher

RESOURCES

Human Rights Campaign – Supporting and caring for transgender children
www.hrc.org

Gender Spectrum
www.genderspectrum.org

Mermaids
www.mermaidsuk.org.uk

Parents of Gender Diverse Children
www.pgdc.org.au

Trans Student Educational Resources
www.transstudent.org

AUTHOR BIO

Jo Hirst is a former primary school teacher and author of *The Gender Fairy*, Australia's first book for transgender children. She wrote *The Gender Fairy* for her own son. Jo works extensively supporting and advocating for families throughout Australia.

Jo grew up in in a family that did not believe in gender stereotyping. Her father was an English teacher with a passion for storytelling and her mother was a builder who loved working with her hands. The two came together to create a happy, supportive and loving environment.

Jo followed in her parents footsteps, studying primary teaching, with a focus on children's literature, and raising a loving family of her own.

Jo lives by the seaside in Melbourne, Australia with her partner and two children.